I0538103

T & A FROM THE WHORROR HOUSE

(TALES& ANECDOTES, WHERE WAS YOUR MIND)

A Whorror House Collection authoured By Lisa Dabrowski

T & A FROM THE WHORROR HOUSE

BY LISA DABROWSKI

A few words on the subject of TRANSGRESSIVE FICTION before I expose you to my work, I am assuming that you already are a fan of it, or have an idea what you might be getting yourself into. Yes TF is shocking to some readers, and the authors who write it are often labeled as rebels, who write TABOO SHIT, covering topics such as dysfunctional family relationships, sexual abuse, sexual freedoms, and the like. The point is we are fearless.

A literary genre that graphically explores such topics as incest and other aberrant sexual practices, mutilation, the sprouting of sexual organs in various places on the human body, urban violence and violence against women, drug use, and highly dysfunctional family relationships, and that is based on the premise that knowledge is to be found at the edge of experience and that the body is the site for gaining knowledge.

The genre has been the subject of controversy, and many forerunners of transgressive fiction, including William S. Burroughs and Hubert Selby Jr., have been the subjects of obscenity trials.

Transgressive fiction shares similarities with splatterpunk, noir, and erotic fiction in its willingness to portray forbidden behaviors and shock readers. But it differs in that protagonists often pursue means to better themselves and their surroundings—albeit unusual and extreme ones. Much transgressive fiction deals with searches for self-identity, inner peace, or personal freedom. Unbound by usual restrictions of taste and literary convention, its proponents claim that transgressive fiction is capable of pungent social commentary.

TWISTED AROUND HER FINGER©

TWISTED AROUND HER FINGER

DANNY

I NOTICED MY SISTER.

WELL, I SHOULDN'T MAKE IT SOUND AS IF I HAD NEVER NOTICED HER BEFORE. OF COURSE I HAD. IN THE PAST, THOUGH, I WAS ONLY AWARE OF HER AS MY KID SISTER, THOUGH: TWO YEARS YOUNGER THAN I, SPOILED AND DISDAINFUL OF PEOPLE WHO WERE LESS ACCOMPLISHED THAN SHE. AS FOR ME, I WAS MOSTLY ABOUT SPORTS: FOOTBALL IN THE FALL AND LACROSSE IN THE SPRING AND BECOMING OBSESSED WITH GIRLS IN GENERAL. NO PLACE IN MY UNIVERSE FOR MY YOUNGER SISTER.

THEN, ONE DAY, I NOTICED HER. TOM, MY BEST FRIEND AND I WERE LAYING BY THE POOL IN OUR BACKYARD, WORKING HARD ON OUR SUNTANS AND DISCUSSING OUR UPCOMING JUNIOR YEAR MOSTLY BECAUSE WE BOTH PLANNED ON BEING VARSITY PLAYERS, AFTER ALL THIS TIME. AS WE LAY THERE, ANGELA CAME OUT TO READ IN THE SUN. AS ALWAYS, SHE TOOK HER PLACE ACROSS THE POOL FROM US AND DIDN'T' SAY A WORD AS SHE PULLED OFF HER SHIRT TO REVEAL HER BIKINI-CLAD BODY.

TOM HADN'T SEEN ANGI SINCE LAST SUMMER AND AS SHE STRIPPED, I HEARD HIS BREATH CATCH, WHICH MADE ME LOOK UP AND TAKE THE FIRST LONG LOOK AT ANGI THAT I HAD TAKEN IN - WELL - EVER. ANGI HAD ALWAYS HAD AN ATHLETIC BODY, WITH A ROUND HARD ASS. IN FACT, MY PARENTS CALLED HER BUBBLE BUTT, SOMETIMES. IN THE

PAST SIX MONTHS THOUGH, UNNOTICED BY ME, SHE HAD ALSO DEVELOPED JUTTING AND FULL BREASTS, AND HER HIPS HAD STARTED TO CURVE ALARMINGLY.

I NOTICED THAT NOT ONLY WAS MY SISTER, BEAUTIFUL, WITH HER MANE OF THICK BLACK HAIR, DARK EYES AND OLIVE SKIN, BUT THAT SHE WAS ALSO NOW IN POSSESSION OF A HEART-STOPPING FIGURE.   AS TOM WOULD SAY, SHE WAS "STACKED".

SHE PAID NO ATTENTION TO US, THOUGH, AND EVENTUALLY TOM HAD TO LEAVE.

AS FOR ME, I WANTED TO TAKE A CLOSER LOOK AT ANGI. I FELT GUILTY ABOUT IT, BUT MY CURIOUSITY AND HER BEAUTY WERE LEADING ME BY MY COCK TOWARDS HER AS SHE LAY ON HER CHAIR, SWEAT POOLING IN HER LONG, DEEP NAVEL.   I SAT DOWN

ANGI, HOW COME YOU DIDN'T SAY HELLO TO TOMMY? THAT WAS RUDE?

SHE OPENED HER EYES AND LOOKED STRAIGHT AT ME AND SAID, HE'S SUCH A CHILD, DANNY.

WHAT DO YOU MEAN? I ASKED SUDDENLY NOTICING THAT DESPITE THE TWO YEAR DIFFERENCE, ANGI WAS SPEAKING TO ME AS IF I MIGHT ALSO BE A CHILD.

IT WAS UNSETTLING IN A WAY. I FELT AS IF I WAS TALKING TO AN ADULT.

HE'S JUST ANOTHER HORNY BOY WITH NOTHING ON HIS MIND OTHER THAN GOING HOME, THINKING OF ME AND MASTURBATING.

I SPUTTERED, AND THOUGH I REALIZED SHE WAS PROBABLY RIGHT, I FELT THE NEED TO REASSERT MY AGE ADVANTAGE AND DEFEND MY FRIEND.

I LAUGHED AND SAID, ANGI, THAT'S SILLY, DENNY HAS A GIRLFRIEND AND HE'S TWO YEARS OLDER THAN YOU ARE. MASTURBATE? ARE YOU CRAZY?

SHE MAINTAINED HER COOL COMPOSURE, AND SAID, IN JUNE, UNCLE SMITH VISITED. DO YOU REMEMBER?

YES, I SAID, SURE.

WHEN I WAS ALONE WITH HIM, HE "ACCIDENTALLY" TOUCHED MY TITS.   I WAS SHOCKED, AND I SLAPPED HIM FULL ACROSS THE FACE AND SAID THAT I WAS GOING TO TELL ON HIM WHEN MOM AND DAD GOT HOME.   HE BEGGED ME NOT TO. HE GOT

ONTO HIS KNEES AND BEGGED ME. IT WAS FUNNY. I FINALLY TOLD HIM THAT I WOULDN'T SAY ANYTHING BUT IT COULD NEVER HAPPEN AGAIN. THE OLD PERVERT KISSED MY FOOT AND THANKED ME AND SCURRIED OFF TO THE GUEST BEDROOM.

ABOUT TEN MINUTES LATER I WENT UP TO GET SOMETHING FROM MY ROOM AND I COULD HEAR HIM JERKING OFF. I'M QUITE SURE THAT I'VE LEARNED A BIT ABOUT MEN IN THE PAST FEW MONTHS.

I DIDN'T KNOW WHAT TO SAY. OH, MY GOD, UNCLE SMITH? HE'S A DOCTOR! HIS WIFE IS BEAUTIFUL! OH, MY GOD! I KEPT SAYING "OH, MY GOD" BUT ON THE OTHER HAND I WAS THRILLED TO BE LET IN ON THIS DIRTY FAMILY SECRET. ANGI GOT UP, STRETCHED, TURNED AND BENT OVER, HER ASS INCHES FROM MY FACE TO PICK UP HER SHIRT AND TOWEL. SHE WENT INTO THE HOUSE, LEAVING ME ALARMED AND PERPLEXED BY THE LARGE HARD ON THAT SHE HAD LOOKED DIRECTLY AT BEFORE SHE WALKED AWAY.

ANGI

THE TRUTH WAS THAT ANGI WAS GLAD THAT UNCLE SMITH HAD TOUCHED HER. SHE REALIZED THAT SHE'D BEEN BOILING FOR MONTHS, AND UNCLE SMITH WAS THE FIRST MAN TO TRY TO HARNESS THE SEXUAL FURY BUILDING UP IN HER. HIS PATHETIC ATTEMPT TO SEDUCE HER WAS THE KEY THAT UNLOCKED HER. STRANGE BUT EQUALLY AMAZING WAS THE FRISSON SHE FELT WHEN SHE JUSTIFIABLY SLAPPED UNCLE ACROSS THE FACE, ESPECIALLY WHEN HE FELL TO HIS KNEES TO GROVEL. THAT WAS MORE THAN A GRATIFYING, IF MISPLACED, "YOU'RE SO SEXY, ANGI": SHE FELT THE HOT RUSH OF POWER IT GAVE HER. IT MADE HER FEEL STRONG AND TOTALLY IN CONTROL AND SHE WAS SURE THAT HAD SHE TOLD UNCLE SMITH TO JERK OFF IN FRONT OF HER, HE WOULD HAVE GLADLY DONE IT.

SHE REALIZED THAT POWER, CONTROL AND SEX COULD BE JOINED. UNCLE SMITH WAS FAR TOO OLD FOR HER PURPOSES, THOUGH, AND MOST BOYS WERE FAR TOO STUPID. AND, TRUTH BE TOLD, SHE HAD LONG HAD A CRUSH ON HER OLDER BROTHER, DANNY. YES, SHE KNEW THAT IT WAS ETHICALLY WRONG – HE WAS HER BROTHER, AFTER ALL

– BUT THEY HAD BEEN CLOSE, WELL, FOREVER, AND IT WAS PRETTY CLEAR SHE WASN'T GETTING OVER HER LOVE OF HIM. ACTUALLY, SHE WAS BEGINNING TO REALIZE NOW THAT HER FEELINGS WERE MORE COMPLEX THAN JUST KID-SISTER ADORATION. WHEN SHE SAW DANNY'S BIG COCK ALL HARD AND SHAMEFUL, SHE FELT THAT SAME RUSHING FEELING SHE'D HAD WHEN SHE MASTURBATED, LATE AT NIGHT. STRANGELY, SHE WAS ALSO EXCITED AT HIS SPUTTERING INABILITY TO HANDLE HER AND HER STORY. SHE FOUND HERSELF WONDERING WHETHER SHE MIGHT TURN DANNY INTO HER LOVER. THEY COULD LEARN FROM ONE ANOTHER IN THE SAFETY AND SECRECY OF ONE ANOTHER – AND IF DANNY WAS LIKE OTHER BOYS – A COMPLETE SLAVE TO HIS COCK – SHE WAS SURE THAT SHE COULD EXPLORE THIS DESIRE TO CONTROL MEN, TOO.

SHE WAS WATCHING DANNY DOWN BY THE POOL, LAYING THERE, FACE RED WITH EMBARRASSMENT. SHE FOUND HERSELF LAUGHING AS SHE REALIZED THAT HE WAS GIVING HIS COCK A STERN TALKING TO – PRESUMABLY ABOUT ITS UNRULY NATURE.

WELL, SHE THOUGHT, NO TIME LIKE THE PRESENT TO TEST THE WATERS A BIT.

SHE WENT INTO THE MASTER BATH, WHICH HAPPENED TO HAVE FULL LENGTH WINDOWS OVERLOOKING THE POOL. SHE STOOD THERE, BEFORE THE WINDOW AND WATCHING DANNY CAREFULLY, SHE PEELED OFF HER BATHING SUIT, AND STOOD THERE WEARING NOTHING OTHER THAN TAN LINES, WAITING FOR DANNY TO LOOK UP.

SHE KNEW SHE WAS SEXY. SHE KNEW IT. TINY WAIST, LONG LEGS, TITS LIKE TWO SOFTBALLS CAPPED WITH FAT, CORAL NIPPLES. LIKE MOTHER, SHE ALSO KEPT HER BUSH NOW THAT SHE COULD GROW ONE. SHE'S DISCOVERED THE INTERNET, AND SHE THOUGHT WOMEN WITH BUSHES WERE SOOO SEXY. AS SHE STOOD THERE, CONTEMPLATING THESE FACTS, DANNY LOOKED UP AND AS HE TRIED TO ADJUST HIS VIEW AGAINST THE GLARE, LIKE SOME GIRAFFE REACHING FOR A DIFFERENT LEAF, HE LOST HIS BALANCE AND FELL ON HIS ASS. BUT NOT BEFORE HE'D SEEN THAT SHE WAS TEASING HER NIPPLES FOR HIM.

SHE KNEW HE'D COME RUNNING. SO EASY TO TURN HIM INTO PUTTY.

BAYOU BABIES©

LISA WAS TRYING TO SOAK AWAY THE STRESSES OF THE DAY IN HOT BATH OF BUBBLES. HER FIFTEEN-YEAR-OLD MIND WAS RACING WITH THOUGHTS OF THE DAY. SHE WAS A SOPHOMORE IN HIGH SCHOOL AND IT WAS FINALS WEEK, AFTER ALL. SHE WAS EXHAUSTED FROM STUDYING, BUT FELT THAT MAINTAINING HER PRISTINE GPA WAS WELL WORTH IT. SHE WAS GOING TO AN IVY LEAGUE SCHOOL, SO HELP HER GOD, AND SHE WAS GOING TO BE RICH AND POWERFUL ONE DAY. HER MOM WAS. THAT WAS HER TEMPLATE. WHY SHOULDN'T SHE BE, TOO?

THE HEAT AND STEAM WERE A BALM, THOUGH, AND AS SHE BEGAN TO RELAX SHE CONSIDERED HER "NEW" BODY. BETH TOOK A MENTAL INVENTORY OF THE CHANGES WROUGHT BY PUBERTY OVER THE PAST TWO YEARS. FIRST, HER BREASTS SEEMED TO HAVE TRIPLED IN SIZE OVERNIGHT AND HER NIPPLES, ONCE BIG, BUT PINK AS CORAL, HAD DARKENED AND THICKENED, PERCEPTIBLY: AGAIN, A REFLECTION OF HER MOTHER. ACTUALLY, WHEN HER BREASTS HAD BEGUN TO GROW, SHE WONDERED WHETHER SHE WAS THE ONLY ONE WHO THOUGHT SUCH PROMINENT NIPPLES WERE ATTRACTIVE, AND SHE HAD WORN INCREASINGLY PADDED BRAS SO THAT THE LARGE AND DARK SHAPE COULDN'T BE DISCERNED EASILY THROUGH HER CLOTHES.

LIKEWISE, HER ONCE OLIVE OYL SHAPE HAD SUDDENLY BECOME VERY LUSH, INDEED. IT SEEMED TO HER THAT OVERNIGHT SHE HAD MORPHED FROM SKINNY AND ATHLETIC, INTO SOME SORT OF SEXUAL CARICATURE, WITH A ROUND, HIGH, DEEPLY CLEFT ASS, AND HIPS OUT OF NOWHERE. WHILE SHE FOUND WOMEN LIKE SALMA HAYEK AND SCARLETT JOHANNSSON TO BE BEAUTIFUL AND SEXY, MOST OF

HER PEERS WERE STILL SKINNY YOUNG GIRLS. SHE FELT DIFFERENT. HER PROMISING SOCCER CAREER WAS SHOT.

STILL, AS SHE CHANGED, IT DID SEEM AS IF MANY OLDER BOYS WERE TAKING A POWERFUL AND NEW INTEREST. HER UNCLE BOB, FOR EXAMPLE, SEEMED TO HAVE LOST THE POWER OF SENSIBLE SPEECH AROUND HER, THE DAY HE CAME OVER TO THE HOUSE AND FOUND HER LAYING BY THE POOL IN LAST YEAR'S BATHING SUIT – A BATHING SUIT WHICH SHE HAD OBSCENELY OUTGROWN – BUT C'MON, SHE WAS AT HOME, NOT IN PUBLIC. SHE HAD NO "INTENT," SHE SIMPLY HADN'T HAD TIME TO GET A NEW BIKINI, AT THAT POINT.

AGAIN, SHE TOOK THE MODEL OF HER MOTHER INTO CONSIDERATION. MOTHER WAS CURVACEOUS AND HAD LARGE, HIGH BREASTS. WHEN BETH THOUGHT OF HER, IT SEEMED AS IF SHE WAS COMPLETELY IN CHARGE OF EVERYONE AND EVERYTHING THAT ENTERED HER ORBIT, INCLUDING FATHER, WHO WHILE BIG AND POWERFUL, WAS A COMPLETELY ADORING LAMB AROUND MOTHER. CONSIDERING UNCLE BOB, MAYBE THIS WAS ALL PERFECTLY NORMAL – CONTROL OF ATTENTIVE MEN.

LISA HAD ALSO BEGUN TO NOTICE THAT ALONG WITH THESE BODILY CHANGES CAME STIRRINGS WITHIN HER THAT SHE DID NOT FULLY UNDERSTAND. SHE FELT ODDLY POWERFUL AND SEXY WHEN UNCLE BOB ACTED LIKE A SPUTTERING FOOL. SHE FELT IN CONTROL AND FOUND HIS FAWNING TO BE PATHETIC, YET AMUSING.

SHE CLOSED HER EYES AND BEGAN TO TOUCH HERSELF INTIMATELY. FEELING HER NIPPLES STIFFEN AS SHE MOVED HER FINGER TIPS OVER THEM FELT LIKE HEAVEN. SHE IMAGINED UNCLE BOB'S REACTION WHEN HE FIRST SAW HER STRAINING THE SEAMS OF LAST YEAR'S BIKINI. UNCLE BOB, SHE DISCOVERED, HAD A FREAKISHLY BIG AND FAT COCK. SHE HAD SEEN IT THICKEN FOR HER, AND ENJOYED THE ASHAMED LOOK ON HIS FACE.

She slipped one finger between her swelling pussy lips to feel the hard bump of her clit, slick with her juices. She groaned, quietly.

Kevin

Lisa's younger brother, Kevin, who was fourteen, was experiencing his own changes, He was a freshman, and like Lisa, he was whip smart. Unlike Lisa, though, he was still a skinny kid: tall and clumsy. Though he was certainly cute enough, he felt awkward around girls and so his interaction with them was largely in fantasy.

In fact, he was painfully shy, and when Lisa had accidentally caught him masturbating, last year, he had turned as red as a beet. He was mortified. He would have been even more mortified, had Lisa known that he was thinking of her body, this being the same day that Uncle Bob came unglued over Lisa's ridiculous bikini.

Matters hadn't been helped with Mother heard the commotion. Lisa had been sent downstairs, and Mother had taken him quietly into her bedroom. There she made him pull his pants down. She explained that he had to learn better self-control, and that she found that discipline was useful in this regard. She then spanked his bottom hot and red with a hair brush.

To his shame and certitude that he was a criminal pervert, he found the attention to be strangely exciting and he came hard, fifteen minutes later in the shower, thinking of Lisa – and his Mother's spanking.

Still, despite his humiliation and the pain of his Mother's whipping, he adored Lisa. As for the masturbation incident, it had somehow bound them closer together especially since Lisa had rubbed some balm into his stinging flesh later that evening, while clucking like a mother hen. That felt so good.

THERE KEVIN STOOD, COCK IN HAND AS HIS SISTER ROSE FORM THE BATH, A GODDESS. SHE STOOD BEFORE HIM, NAKED AND DRIPPING AND KEVIN DIDN'T EVEN HAVE THE SENSE TO MOVE HIS HAND OFF OF HIS COCK. IF ANYTHING, HER REGAL, SHAMELESS NUDITY ONLY MADE HIS COCK GROW HARDER.

SHE STOOD THERE, LEGS SLIGHTLY SPREAD, HANDS ON HIPS. KEVIN COULD SEE THAT HER PUSSY LIPS WERE SHAVED, AND HER BEAUTIFUL TRIMMED BUSH WAS DRIPPING WATER ONTO HER PUFFY LIPS.

LISA

THE AIR FELT COOL ON HER SKIN. INVIGORATING, BUT NOT SO EXCITING AS CATCHING HER YOUNGER BROTHER JERKING HIS BIG FAT COCK WHILE STARING AT HER. CLEARLY, KEVIN WAS GROWING UP, BECAUSE WHILE STILL SKINNY, HIS COCK WAS NOW A THICK, HEALTHY 7 INCHES (AND GROWING?). HER MIND RACED WITH CONFUSED THOUGHTS. PERHAPS THERE WAS AN OPPORTUNITY HERE THAT SHE SHOULD TAKE ADVANTAGE OF?

"OH, MY GOD, YOU LITTLE PERVERT, WHAT ARE YOU DOING SPYING ON ME?"

KEVIN STOOD THERE, CONFUSED HIMSELF AND BEGAN TO SPUTTER

"I'M SO SORRY. I'M SO SORRY, LISA...I WAS JUST WALKING BY AND I SAW YOU IN THE TUB, TOUCHING YOURSELF, AND I COULDN'T HELP IT. YOU'RE SO BEAUTIFUL."

"HOW DARE YOU MASTURBATE IN FRONT OF ME, KEVIN? DIDN'T YOU LEARN ANYTHING FROM THE WHIPPING MOM GAVE YOU?"

LISA SLAPPED KEVIN'S FACE AND HE TOOK HIS HAND AWAY FROM HIS COCK, BUT SHE NOTICED THAT THE STINGING SLAP, IF ANYTHING, ONLY MADE KEVIN'S COCK BIGGER AND FATTER. SHE MARVELED AT HOW BEAUTIFUL IT WAS AND HOW IT MADE HER FEEL DOWN LOW IN HER PUSSY. WAS SHE DRIPPING? THE THRILL SHE FELT FROM SLAPPING KEVIN SENT A FRISSON OF EXCITEMENT FROM HER NIPPLES DIRECTLY TO HER CLIT. SHE FELT LIKE TOUCHING HERSELF AGAIN.

"GOOD BOY.

"I DON'T WANT YOU TO NEED PUNISHMENT, TO BE A GOOD BOY, KEVIN, BUT YOU MUST BE OBEDIENT. DO YOU UNDERSTAND? "

"I KNOW LISA BUT I WAS THINKING ABOUT HOW BEAUTIFUL YOU ARE AND FOR SOME REASON I WAS THINKING OF MOTHER PUNISHING ME, AND..WELL...I'M SO ASHAMED. WHAT'S WRONG WITH ME"?

A TEAR STREAMED DOWN KEVIN'S FACE AND BETH FELT NOTHING BUT LOVE FOR HIM AND GENTLY TOOK HIM INTO HER ARMS. KEVIN SNUFFLED, BUT BETH FELT THE HARDNESS OF HIS COCK AGAINST HER BELLY AND IT MADE HER NIPPLES STIFF.

SHE REALIZED THAT THIS WAS THE PERFECT OPPORTUNITY: SHE LOVED KEVIN AND KNEW THAT SHE COULD EXPLORE HER BUDDING SEXUALITY WITH HIM IN A SAFE ENVIRONMENT. SHE ALSO KNEW THAT SHE HUNGERED TO EXPLORE MANY OF THE DARK FANTASIES THAT CLOUDED HER MIND, AND WHEN KEVIN GOT EVEN MORE EXCITED BY HER SLAP AND HUMILIATION, SHE REALIZED THAT OPPORTUNITY WAS KNOCKING.

SHE STOOD BACK FROM KEVIN.

"KEVIN, DO YOU THINK I'M BEAUTIFUL?"

KEVIN LOOKED AS IF HE WAS STRUCK BY LIGHTNING. HE NODDED, MUTELY.

LISA SLAPPED HIS FACE AGAIN AND SAID, "ANSWER ME, KEVIN, AND CALL ME MISS LISA WHEN YOU DO."

"YES, MISS LISA, YOU'RE THE MOST BEAUTIFUL GIRL, I'VE EVER SEEN, MISS LISA".

"GOOD. VERY GOOD. DO YOU WANT TO KISS ME, KEVIN?"

"OH, GOD YES, MISS LISA". KEVIN BEGAN TO LEAN FORWARD.

LISA LAUGHED AT HOW EASILY KEVIN WAS BEING LED. HE WAS ADORABLE.

"NO, KEVIN, GET ON YOUR KNEES."

KEVIN LOOKED CONFUSED BUT HE FELL DOWN NEVERTHELESS, AS COMMANDED, HIS SHORTS IN A PILE AROUND HIS ANKLES.

"KEVIN, I'M ONLY GOING TO ASK YOU THIS ONCE: DO YOU WANT TO BE MY SLAVE BOY? DO YOU WANT TO EXPLORE YOUR SEXUALITY WITH ME? WILL YOU DO ANYTHING I COMMAND, WITHOUT SHAME OR HESITATION?"

KEVIN WOULD HAVE AGREED TO ANYTHING AT THAT POINT AND SO OF COURSE HE SAID, "YES, MISS LISA, YES, MISS LISA, YES MISS LISA"?

"GOOD BOY".

LISA TURNED AROUND, AND LOOKING OVER HER SHOULDER, TAPPED HER FULL, ROUND, FIRM ASS CHEEK WITH ONE FINGER.

"SLAVE, YOU MAY KISS MY ASS, NOW. JUST KNOW THAT FROM NOW ON, WHEN YOU GREET ME AS MY SLAVE, YOU WILL BE EXPECTED TO WORSHIP MY ASS BEFORE ANYTHING ELSE. WOULD YOU LIKE THAT SLAVE?"

HIS VOICE TREMBLING, KEVIN SAID "YES, MISS LISA"

BETH REACHED BEHIND HER WITH BOTH HANDS AND ARCHED HER BACK AS SHE SPREAD HER CHEEKS.

"LICK, SLAVE".

KEVIN LEANED FORWARD AS IF PREPARING TO TOUCH A PRICELESS OBJECT OF ART. HE STUDIED THE PERFECTION OF HER FLAWLESS ASS, THE WAY HER ASSHOLE DARKENED AND PUCKERED. HE FELT THE HEAT OF HER SKIN AND WETNESS FROM THE BATH. HE SCENTED THE WETNESS OF HER PUSSY. HE KISSED HER ASSHOLE DEEPLY AND REVERENTLY AND THEN BEGAN TO LICK HER ASS DEEPLY IN THE MOST ABJECT WORSHIP.

As for Lisa, she was in heaven. Kevin was licking her so lovingly, so ardently. She felt her wetness streaming down the insides of her legs. Kevin would do anything...anything, that she wanted him to do. That much was clear. She dropped a finger to her clit and touched it, and she came hard, her ass cheeks clutching Kevin's face like a vise.

Love At Last

Later that night a violent storm brewed outside. Thunder roared and lightening lit up the skies. A fierce wind howled outside her window, making branches scrape against the siding and her window.

Lisa was terrified of storms. She had always been afraid of them, but now, she realized that she needn't be alone and afraid. She was wearing a pair of thin cotton panties and a cut off t-shirt, but as she scurried to her brother's room, she didn't think Kevin would mind.

She tip toed down the hall to his room, not wanting her parents to hear her footsteps in their bedroom downstairs. Gently she turned the doorknob and entered her brother's room. In one quiet and smooth move, she slid into his bed, and snuggled up to him, pressing her lush ass against him. To her surprise, Kevin was naked. Why the shameless slut!

She felt better. She felt excited.

Instinctually, Kevin though still asleep, grumbled a bit, and then rolled over, spooning Lisa's curvy frame. He began to awake, but only in part. He felt as if he were dreaming: the smell of Lisa's hair; the feel of her ample bottom against his cock. He felt himself beginning to get hard.

Beth felt it as well, and like a gardener nurturing a new flower, she carefully rubbed her ass against him, and reaching down between her legs, got her wetness on a finger and wiped it on the back of her neck so that her new pet dog could get the scent of the prize.

Kevin groaned, by now his cock swaddled between Lisa's ass cheeks, skin separated from skin by only the most soft and paper-thin cotton.

KEEPING HER ASS TO HIM, LISA TURNED HER UPPER BODY TOWARDS KEVIN AND LICKED HIS LIPS. KEVIN GROANED AGAIN AND AWOKE, TO KISS HIS MISS LISA DEEPLY. LISA SUCKED HIS TONGUE INTO HER MOUTH, AND RAN HER HAND INTO HIS HAIR, GRIPPING HIM TIGHTLY BY THE ROOTS.

LOOKING LOVINGLY INTO HIS EYES, LISA SAID, "LICK SLAVE", AND PULLED HIS HEAD IN THE RIGHT DIRECTION. LISA NEARLY SWOONED WHEN KEVIN SAID, "YES, MISS LISA" AND SLIPPED DOWN UNTIL HIS FACE WAS FLUSH WITH HER ASS. FIRST HE KISSED HER BOTTOM THOROUGH THE COTTON, BUT THEN BETH PULLED IT DOWN SO THAT HER BROTHER COULD LICK HER DEEPLY AS HE HAD THAT AFTERNOON.

SHE FELT A FURNACE GROWING IN HER PUSSY AND COMMANDED KEVIN TO STOP. SHE ROLLED ONTO HER BACK AND TOOK HER PANTIES ALL THE WAY OFF, AND SAID, "IT'S TIME FOR YOU TO LEARN TO PLEASE YOUR MISTRESS, BY LICKING HER PUSSY, SLAVE".

OBEDIENCE

EAGERLY KEVIN LAPPED AT HER SWEETNESS. HE LICKED HER DEEPLY SHOVING HIS TONGUE DEEP INTO HER SOAKED, SILKEN PUSSY. LISA ARCHED HER MOUND UP TO MEET HIS MOUTH, HER THROBBING CLIT ENGORGED WITH EXCITEMENT. SHE REACHED DOWN AND HELD HIS HEAD TIGHTLY IN PLACE, AND BEGAN TO RIDE HIS FACE, GRINDING HER BLOOD-ENGORGED PUSSY AGAINST KEVIN'S CHIN, MOUTH AND TONGUE.

ALL THE WHILE SHE FELT HER BROTHER'S FAT COCK RUBBING AGAINST HER LEG, AND THIS ONLY ADDED TO HER PLEASURE. SHE KNEW THAT SHE WAS THE ONE THAT HE WORSHIPPED AND ADORED. SHE WAS THE REASON FOR HIS NOW DRIPPING COCK. SHE CAME AGAIN.

By the time she came for the third time, she was marveling at Kevin's obedience and eagerness to please her. By that time the storm had passed. She slipped out of the bed and pulled the sheets back to expose her brother's swollen and drooling cock to the moonlight which now beamed across the bed. She felt a hunger to have that cock deep in her; to ride it and feel it crush against her cervix. Ah, but that would only make Kevin her lover and her fuck toy. And he wanted so much more. She knew she could have as much handsome cock as she pleased, but she wanted to plunge into darker waters and she knew that Kevin required training for that voyage.

Kevin looked up at her; the love and adoration clear as the moonlight in his eyes. Lisa stood there, hands on hips, considering. She was naked, save for the cut off top, and she knew that he could see the swell of her jutting under-breasts. She knew what it was doing to him as he gently reached to touch.

"Slave, you are not allowed to ever touch me without permission. Do you understand?" Without awaiting an answer she pointed to the hard wooden floor and said "get on your knees."

Kevin, looking forlorn and terribly horny, slid from the bed and assumed a position of obedience. Lisa had an idea. "Stay, boy", she said and walked from the room and gently down the stairs.

Slipping by her Mother's room, she saw that it was lit by candle-light, and as she silently peered in, she glanced her Mother standing at the foot of the bed. She was naked and as always Lisa was struck by her beauty. She was wearing opera length gloves, black thigh boots, with high heels and a thin black belt cinched around her waist. She was nude otherwise, her breasts, even bigger than Lisa's jutted out lewdly. She couldn't see Daddy, but when Mother

TURNED A BIT SHE SAW THAT RATHER THAN NUDE, SHE WAS WEARING A BIG STRAP ON COCK.

LISA WOULD HAVE LIKED TO STAY AND SILENTLY WATCH AND LEARN, BUT KEVIN WAITED. LISA STOLE TO THE LAUNDRY ROOM AND FOUND WHAT SHE WAS LOOKING FOR AND RETURNED TO FIND KEVIN STILL ON HIS KNEES.

LISA APPROACHED HIM FROM BEHIND AND STROKING HIS HEAD, SHE SAID "SUCH A GOOD BOY", AND BEGAN TO PLACE THE COLLAR AROUND HIS NECK, WHICH SHE THEN ATTACHED TO A LONG DOG LEASH.
"SLAVE, YOU WILL NEED OBEDIENCE TRAINING. YOU WILL NEED DISCIPLINE. YOU ARE EAGER, BUT I REQUIRE MUCH MORE THAN EAGERNESS, IF YOU WISH TO BE MY GOOD BOY. DO YOU WISH TO BE MY GOOD BOY?"

KEVIN, GROANED WITH NEED AND SAID, "YES, MISS LISA, I WANT TO MAKE YOU HAPPY".

"HMMM, WELL, BOY, WHAT WOULD MAKE ME HAPPY RIGHT NOW IS TO WATCH YOU JACK YOUR COCK FOR ME".

KEVIN DID AS COMMANDED, THOUGH IT WAS CLEAR THAT HE HAD BEEN HOPING FOR MORE CONTACT WITH LISA'S BODY. IT WAS DELICIOUS FOR LISA TO WATCH HIM MASTURBATE HIMSELF ON COLLAR AND LEASH: DELICIOUS TO FEEL THE POWER OF KNOWING THAT HER BROTHER WAS FALLING EVER MORE DEEPLY IN THRALL TO HER. IT WAS PROFOUNDLY EXCITING ON AN EVIL LEVEL TO KNOW THAT WHATEVER SHE IMAGINED, NO MATTER HOW PERVY, KEVIN WOULD EAGERLY DO – IF PROPERLY TRAINED.

LISA REACHED DOWN AS KEVIN CONTINUED TO JACK HIS COCK AND BEGAN TO PINCH HIS NIPPLES. HARDER AND HARDER SHE PINCHED, KNOWING HOW PAINFUL IT WAS. "DARLING, YOU NEED TO LEARN TO CRAVE PAIN AND PLEASURE, FOR ME. THAT WILL PLEASE ME. DO YOU UNDERSTAND?"

KEVIN RESPONDED "YES, MISS LISA. I UNDERSTAND."

"Now be a good boy and cum for Mistress".

Kevin responded by spraying long arcs of hot jism a good 3 feet onto the bed.

Lisa said, "Good boy, now get in bed" and Kevin slipped into his jism soaked sheets.

"You may now kiss me good night, slave," said Lisa, turning her ass to him and bending slightly for Kevin to hungrily lick her asshole.

Lisa returned to her room feeling very happy, and not the least bit scared of storms, anymore.

Mistress Fucks Her Slave

Lisa was certain that her Mother's Strap-On played a large part in her relationship with her Father. She understood, at a very basic level, that fucking Father in the ass was a critical part of establishing ownership.

Now, she fantasized about using Mommy's strap on, on Kevin, to fuck him would be essential in the obedience training. She needed to make him crave her even more than he did now, if that was even possible.

Mother kept her toys in the second drawer of her nightstand, and they were going away for the weekend, leaving her and Kevin to their own devices. Lisa knew that this would be the perfect opportunity to take his virginity!

Her clit quickened at the thought.

After seeing their parents off for the weekend, Beth and Kevin looked at each other knowingly.

"Kevin, you want to prove your loyalty to Miss Lisa, don't you?" she asked with a wicked grin

"Yes, Miss Lisa," he answered with a soulful whine.

"Good boy. Now strip."

Kevin removed his clothes as directed, and Lisa was amused by the fact that his cock was already thickening. She decided that it was time to inspect her property.

"Slave, put your hands on top of your head and spread your legs a bit...Miss Lisa wants to inspect you".

KEVIN DID AS DIRECTED, AND LISA WALKED SLOWING AROUND HIM, INSPECTING HIM AS SHE WOULD A HORSE THAT SHE WAS CONSIDERING FOR PURCHASE. HER HAND FLOWED OVER HIS BELLY AND FLANKS. SHE SQUEEZED HIS ASS, TESTING ITS FIRMNESS.

"BEND, SLAVE".

KEVIN BENT AT THE WAIST AND LISA CUPPED HIS BALLS IN HER HAND, FEELING THEIR WEIGHT.

"SLAVE, YOU DO UNDERSTAND THAT YOUR BALLS ARE MINE, YES? THAT YOU MAY NOT CUM UNLESS I GIVE YOU PERMISSION? YOU UNDERSTAND THIS?"

KEVIN SAID "YES, MISS LISA"

WITH THAT, LISA SLAPPED KEVIN'S ASS SO HARD THAT IT HURT HER HAND, AND LEFT A FURIOUS RED HAND-PRINT ON HER BROTHER'S ASS.

KEVIN WAS SILENT.

LISA WAS PLEASED.

NOW GET ON YOUR KNEES AND CRAWL INTO MOTHER'S ROOM," SHE ORDERED WHILE ATTACHING A COLLARED LEASH.

OBEDIENTLY KEVIN CRAWLED ON ALL FOURS ALONGSIDE HER INTO THEIR PARENTS' BEDROOM. LISA ATTACHED HIS LEASH TO THE FOOT OF THE BED.

GOING TO THE CLOSET, SHE TOOK OUT ONE OF HER MOTHER'S STRAP ON COCKS.

LISA SLOW STRIPPED DOWN NOTHING, THE LIGHT IN KEVIN'S EYES A BURNING FIRE.

KEVIN WATCHED WITH THE MOST DELICIOUS LOOK OF FEAR AND HUNGER IN HIS EYES, AS SHE CINCHED THE STRAPS ON AND THE LEATHER BIT INTO HER TANNED AND FIRM FLESH.

"KEVIN, DARLING, YOU MAY THINK OF THIS AS OUR WEDDING, NIGHT. I'M GOING TO TAKE YOUR VIRGINITY. NOW BE A GOOD BOY AND GET UP ON THE BED. STAY ON YOUR KNEES BUT HOLD YOUR HANDS BEHIND YOUR BACK".

KEVIN OBEYED AND HE FELT HIS HANDS BOUND TOGETHER. HE COULDN'T SEE LISA, BUT HE HEARD HER RUMMAGING AND THEN HE REALIZED THAT SHE HAD FOUND A BALL GAG.

"LOVE, BE A LAMB AND LET MY PUT THIS ON YOU. I WANT TO HEAR YOU GROAN, BUT I DON'T WANT THE NEIGHBORS TO HEAR US PLAYING".

HIS SISTER PUT THE GAG ON HIM.

SHE STOOD BEHIND HIM AND SHE RAN HER HAND OVER HIS ASS, AND BALLS AND SHE GENTLY FINGERED HIS ASSHOLE. IT ALL FELT SOOO GOOD.

"DOESN'T THAT FEEL NICE, SLAVE? I CAN TELL BY YOUR UNRULY COCK THAT YOU LIKE BEING AT YOUR SISTER'S MERCY. DON'T YOU?"

KEVIN COULD ONLY GRUNT YES.

"DARLING, MISTRESS NEEDS TO TRAIN YOU, THOUGH. TO MAKE YOU UNDERSTAND THAT WITH PLEASURE COMES OBEDIENCE AND THAT ONLY COMES FROM YOU LEANING TO ACCEPT MISTRESS'S PAIN LIKE A GOOD BOY".

PASSING THE CROSS©

Gaunt and weary from surviving in the wasteland of the desert, Jesus was looking forward to his meeting with Lucifer atop the mountain. Perhaps they could end their conflict without any more pain, he didn't have the energy within him to endure nor expel more hate.

The winds grazed the blistered skin of Jesus, the biting chill brought relief to with its sting as he made his way to the summit of the mountain. Looking ahead he could see the figure of Lucifer, smiling down at him with a suspicious note of compassion in his eye that could only mean an ulterior motive was lurking.

"Come, My Brother," Lucifer said, putting his arm around Jesus, "Look at this world. The splendour of it. This should be yours, to have dominion over. This is your garden, and you the constant gardener, the leader of all men. You are after all, King of Kings."

Atop the summit of this mountain you could see the world and all its glory. Flora and fauna, rivers and streams. In the blink of an eye all ugliness faded into darkness. The Angels of Light had illuminated the world.

"All of this was meant to be yours. You are truly the King of Kings and this is your domain by which to rule over. All of the Land and Sea faring creatures are yours and they bow down to you, My Lord. The fragrant blooms and fresh fruit that they produce all belong to you. You hold power over it all. Every creature great and small you hold at your will, "Lucifer said to a weary Jesus.

Looking around Jesus admired the beauty that surrounded him. The smells that perfumed the air. Birds soaring high above him and small animals burrowing below him. The world was a beautiful place indeed. A Kingdom worthy to rule over. He swelled with pride knowing that this was his domain.

His arm still around Christ's shoulder, Lucifer continued to speak." You have been persecuted far too long, and for all the wrong reason my brother. The time has come for you to come into the life your Father intended you to have. To rule over His Kingdom. To be King of Kings. You do realize that if you go back into town they will crucify you. You will be nailed to a cross for spreading the word of your Father. This is not justice and it surely is not what your Father wants for you. He wants you to live! To rule over his Kingdom! I however have never truly been brought to justice for that fight I started in Heaven. Let me trade places with you. I can go back to town in your place. Then I will finally pay the price for what I have done, and you can claim your inheritance, this spacious Kingdom."

Filled with pride, perhaps one of the sneakiest and deadliest of the seven deadly sins, Jesus agreed to Lucifer's proposition. Why shouldn't he have what was right fully due him? His Father had created this Perfect Kingdom, a literal heaven on Earth, and all he had known of it was suffering, pain and persecution. It was time for him to be Lord and master to Rule over the Kingdom and everything in it, all creatures great and small. This was his true destiny he thought, to be King of Kings. A King is nothing without a Queen so he asked Lucifer for just one thing before he sent him back to take his place, to send the whore Mary of Magdalene to be his wife. Lucifer was well pleased with this choice, and agreed gleefully.

Judas, having left what was to be the final gathering of Christ's closest friends and family. Ran with conflict in his heart. He could see past the mask that Lucifer was wearing, exposing him for his true self. In a desperate act of love for his Saviour he turned Jesus into authorities as an instigator, an enemy of the state. A meeting was set up where he would point him out by giving him a customary kiss where Christ and his followers were gathered in the Garden. Others close to Christ had mixed feelings as well that Lucifer glibly explained away, Thomas and peter among them. Judas led the guards to him in the Garden that night, and with a kiss, they knew who to detain at once.

Lucifer was nailed to the cross, crucified in Christ's place. Jesus' mother wept at his feet. The whore Mary also shed tears. Lucifer told the Sinners next to him that they would receive the kingdom as well as him that day; of course he neglected to specify which kingdom they would be receiving.

Looking up, with the makeshift crown of thorns that had been placed upon his head, Lucifer uttered the words "Forgive them Father for they know not what they do, "and he smiled inside because he knew that was true. The ground began to tremble, and the sky darkened. Once again Lucifer glanced above and muttered "It is done," The earth burst open below, the sky became dark as night, and claps of thunder made a roar.

Three days had passed and the whore Mary of Magdalene went to the tomb to take care of Christ's body. She noticed the stone had been removed and was upset when she peered in and did not find Jesus' body lying there. Lucifer came to her with a finger over his mouth, as if to tell her to be quiet. "Do not cry Mary of Magdalene. Jesus waits for you to be his Queen and sail away with him. He has chosen you to birth his children and to rule dominion over his Father's Kingdom with him. He awaits you on the hilltop. Go to him."

Mary went to Jesus and the sailed away together. They started a family, and lived a life of nobility in Europe. Happy and content, they lived amongst their people, in their church, a part of their church, with and without their church. They lived a life full of love and passion for one another.

Lucifer having died and ascended ushered in the prophecy of those visions of the sages. Everyone sits around and waits for John's Revelation to happen, but what they don't realize is that it has already happened. He wasn't telling the future, he was tripping on the past. The day Lucifer turned The Garden of Eden into Hell.

The Clown Father by Lisa Dabrowski®

Nunzio grew up in the mountains of Italy without the benefit of any parents. Life was not kind to him, having watched his mother and father slain at the hands of the village Patron; he fled to the safety of the wilderness and his own devices for survival, swearing one day to exact revenge one day on the man that had stolen his name from him.

A sect of Franciscan Monks found Nunzio and took him in. They provided the essentials of life for him, food, shelter, clothing, and a Catholic upbringing. They could not however remove the hatred from his heart for the Patron. The monks were not a glum lot, they enjoyed giving freely of themselves and part of their ministry was to visit the sick and dying to spread cheer and comfort. They found that applying colourul face paint, and acting the part of a clown enhanced the visits for the sick children. They encouraged Nunzio to participate in these activities with them. To give freely of one's self and to love thy neighbour as thyself was after all part of their missionary work. Nunzio discovered he had freedom behind the mask of face paint. He could move about undetected, no one knowing his identity, so long as he remained dressed in the colourful attire and face paint. His mind soon worked on ways of exacting revenge on the Patron for his parents and this was going to afford him the opportunity.

Nunzio decided to apply a full clown mask when dressing for his visits into the village. He knew that he was not welcome in the village by the Patron, and it was in this manner he had the freedom to move about undetected in the village. Instead of thinking about all the good he could do with his mission work with the friars, his mind wandered to thoughts of revenge against the man who had brutally murdered his parents.

On one of their jaunts to the hospital, Nunzio. In full costume, wandered off from the children's ward with his basket of wooden puppets he made to give out to the children. Peering into the rooms of the older patients, he couldn't help but look twice at one in particular, it was the Patron himself. This was an opportunity he could not pass up. Knowing that he could enter his room, with a welcome smile, was simply far too much to ask for.

Nunzio positioned a wooden doll at the foot of The Patron's bed. Gleefully the puppet danced about the edge of the bed putting on a show for the older man. Deftly, Nunzio introduced two more puppets to the show, a couple; they appeared to be a happy couple in love. The Patron was enjoying the show, and clapping along. All at once the happy couples were struck down by the dancing puppet, and fell to the floor. A smaller puppet, carved to look like a court jester appeared by the Dancer, pushing him to the floor. Nunzio sprung up from the end of the bed where he had been working the dolls. He glared into The Patron's black eyes. This was his opportunity and he was going to seize it. Taking the old man's pillow he put it over his face and took his last breath from him just the way he had took it from his parents. Nunzio felt a rush having the power over life and death, and suddenly realized what it must be like to be The Patron.

The Order, having realized what he had done, thought it in Nunzio's best interest to send him abroad to one of their friends in the United States. He was sent to reside with Father O'Shea. A fine upstanding Irish Catholic Priest, whom they thought would instill the fear of God himself in Nunzio. Perhaps they had been to lacking in the discipline department they thought to themselves. Father O'Shea certainly suffered no fools and would whip him into shape, if he could be whipped into shape that is.

Father O'Shea put Nunzio up his house along with his housekeeper, a delightful middle aged woman that click clacked when she walked. Nunzio adored Miss Sophie. She had salt and pepper hair that she always kept twisted upon her hair, and she always smelled of cinnamon. She was a baking woman, always in the kitchen, and Nunzio loved to hide out in there with her.

One afternoon Miss Sophie asked Nunzio to help her peels and slice apples for pies that she was making for the church social. Holding the knife in his hand brought back the memories of the puppets he used to carve in Italy, and subsequently the puppet show he put on for The Patron. His mind began to wander. He could feel that rush in his veins, having control over life and death. To hold that power in your hands. He realized that the knife also wielded the same power as that pillow. He would dress up for the church social and use this knife he thought to himself. He continued slicing apples, whistling while he did so.

Sneaking into Miss Sophie's room, Nunzio was on the prowl for face paint. She had white face concealer, red lipsticks, rouges, blue and green eye shadow, and mascara. These would have to do he thought to himself. I will paint myself up nicely with these, most women don't realize how much of this paint they actually wear until they see it on a clown anyway he thought to himself.

The next day the parish was a flurry of activity, everyone buzzing about getting ready for the church social and bazaar. Nunzio was in his room after setting up Miss Sophie's table of pies, staring at himself in his bureau mirror. He was taken aback by the glint in his eyes. He had seen that shimmer before. The look of power, the look of madness, the look of The Patron. Nunzio was morphing into The Patron.

The white concealer was applied first, then a healthy dose of rouge on the cheeks. Diamonds of Liquid Black Eye Liner were drawn around his eyes. He filled them in with alternating shades of blue and green eye shadow. Now for the mouth. He wanted this to be just right. From cheek to cheek he outlined an impish grin, and then filled it in with cherry red lipstick. Giving himself the once over just one more time, he realized something was missing. He scurried off to Father O'Sheas room and grabbed one of his robes. Donning the black frock and white collar now made his ensemble complete. He cackled wickedly. I am The Clownfather.

Nunzio could hear the parishioners drifting into the hall. He looked at the blade of his knife; in the glimmer of the silver he caught a distorted reflection of himself. Was this distortion the final thing people would see once The Clownfather paid them a visit? Where was he? Nunzio felt himself drifting away, far away to the night his parents had died. He often wondered if had died that night as well. The good part of him anyway. The redeemable part. The Clownfather was beyond redemption, he was thirsty, and the only thing that could quench that thirst was power. The power of life of death. Blood!

Creeping down the back stairs, Nunzio went to the basement and had a healthy glass of Father O'Sheas Irish Whiskey before making his way to the church hall. He felt a wee bit woozy, perhaps he drank too much on an empty stomach, or maybe he should have stuck to the wine. A dizzy knife wielding clown couldn't be a good thing he thought to himself. Feeling like he was going to drop at any moment, he decided to go the kitchen and put something in his stomach. A piece of Soda bread might do the trick. There it was in the breadbox, a blade sharper and much longer than the one he had. Slicing a thick chunk of bread, he realized that this was the knife he was going to use. He crammed the bread in his mouth, trying desperately to sober himself up. He wiped the blade clean, he wanted it to sparkle and shine. At last a mirror reflection in the blade. Perfection. Now if he only his stomach would settle.

He tucked the knife securely in the back of his pants at his belt loop and made his way down the corridor to the church hall. The Social was in full swing now; He could hear laughter and music filling the air. The smells of the parish ladies cooking hung low in the halls. The mixture was making his stomach churn even more. There was a rubbish can midway down the hall, he stopped and hurled the whiskey, bread and possibly his toe nails as well before continuing on. He felt somewhat sober now.

The doors to the hall were now in front of him. Nunzio stood there staring into his knife, reflecting the look of power staring back at him. The One who holds the power of life and death in hands with a swift wield of the blade, the person staring back at him was The Clownfather. Standing outside the doors he could hear Miss Sophie laughing with the other women of the parish, and carryon with idle gossip the way women do when they gather. They sounded like a bunch of cackling hens he thought to himself, cackling hens that would make a good pot of chicken and dumplings. Father O'Shea and his booming roar could be heard clear down the hall. Sounds like he's been nipping the Irish whiskey already. Nunzio wondered how Father O'Shea could consume so much of the liquor without hurling up his toe nails. Today The Clownfather would show Father O'Shea that there is someone new in town.

Transformed into The Clownfather, Nunzio entered into the side entrance of the parish social hall undetected. This was how he had planned it. To move about freely, undetected. Hidden behind the mask of makeup. A Clown that no one takes seriously until they are forced to take seriously. The underdog who bites back. The smallest of small wielding the power of life and death in the palm of his hand.

Purveying the crowd from around the corner, he felt his pulse race and the blood once again rush to his head making him dizzy. This was a different kind of dizziness, a flurry of a rush, the kind he experienced when he kissed Mary Jane in the alley behind the parish. A million butterfly wings brushing up against his belly at once tickling him from inside. The incomparable feeling of lust and tender love, yes, the thought of drawing blood to the point of death gave him this feeling.

Standing in the corner he could see a group of neighborhood thugs who had made time with his sweet Mary Jane. They were definitely going to feel the wrath of The Clownfather today. Mr. Jones who came to confession every Saturday to wipe away the sins of the past week. All the rot he had done cheating his boss, skimming off the books, not to mention his affair with Miss Evelyn. That fat bastard was a pig ripe for poking. Decisions, decisions, where to start? This was the quandary Nunzio found himself in. They were all two faced hypocrites worthy of the blade. Evangelize and her group of hangers on, now they surely deserved a good gutting, after the shameless way they paraded up down the hallways of school, lifting their skirts for any athlete who would pay them the slightest bit of attention. How was he going to do the most damage in the shortest amount of time? This was the dilemma he found himself in. A predicament indeed.

Wisdom , albeit it skewered, Nunzio decided he would save Father O'Shea for last. Making the Good Shepard watch his flock get slaughtered one by one added to his amusement. Thinking of Father O'Shea as the Good Shepard actually made his stomach churn, here was a man who offered absolution, guidance for troubled youth, and this was his public persona. Behind closed doors he carried on a lewd affair with a young mother he counseled that suffered not only the affliction of addiction but had the misfortune of birthing a bastard child fathered by an incarcerated pedophile. You are supposed to pray for those in your Parish, not Prey upon them.

Purveying the crowd, Nunzio walked through them passing out smiley face cookies to those who would laugh and clap for him. A few did the sign of the cross to him, Evangelize even asked him to forgive her of her sins. She would be finding absolution soon and swiftly he thought to himself. Miss Sophie and he coop of cackling hens roared with laughter at him. Tears streaming down their faces they were laughing so hard and boisterously. Tears of laughter would turn to tears of terror. Nunzio looked down at his shoes, he had on a pair of Father O' Sheas' shoes , he had stuffed the toes with newspaper for a better fit, and they were still a bit floppy. Big old floppy clown shoes he thought to himself. The only thing that these shoes were missing was a splattering of blood.

" Tears Of A Clown " by Smokey Robinson was playing on the phonograph and through the Social Hall sound system, it was time for The Clownfather to strike.

The Jocks with all their raging masculinity. Their life was lived through their dicks. Hell they were nothing more than walking, talking dicks. Pricks whothought because they scored on the field, they should score high on a test and above all else score with the girls. The Clownfather knew where to make the cut on that team. Right where it hurt. Looking Bill, John and Ted right square in the eye, he took his knife and stabbed away at their penises. While they were bent over in pain, he went for the neck slashing the jugular vein. Dicks, that was too easy. Time for The Spirit Squad!

Evangelize , Torri, Alice, and Mary were hovered together in a dark corner giggling. Their perky breasts jutting out of their cashmere sweaters. Gossiping away about the plain girls who didn't make the squad, and had no life, other than making good grades. The good girls. The insufferable sluts! So vain, all made up too, thought they belonged on the cover of the latest fashion magazine. These bitches clearly had no heart at all. The Clownfather would strike right in the heart. Their cold heart. Mary had teased him with kissing and fondling in the alley, she would get the first blow. Smiling in her face , He took his knife and plunged it deep within her chest cavity until blood cascaded down onto the tips of his shoes. Swiftly he followed suit with Alice, Tori and Evangelize. Once again going for the jugular vein before he moved on.

He adored Miss Sophie , and was in conflict over what he was about to do. Realizing that she was a mere gossip clucking away like a cackling hen with the lot of the ladies auxiliary, he justified his actions. Listen to them over there judging everyone in the parish. Who did they think they were to sit in judgment of all those young mothers out there trying to find crumbs to stick in their children's mouths. Fat Hens cackling away. A fat hen deserves to be cut up and put in a pot. All cooped up together over there. The seven of them. The Clownfather went up behind them one by one slicing them in the back of the neck, then severing their jugular vein,. Cackle no more you hens! He felt a twinge of remorse for Miss Sophie, bending over he kissed her goodbye as she lay on the floor bleeding out.

Little Girl Lost, Father O'Shea's Mistress was stoned and all alone up by the punch bowl, Gazing down into as if the orange slices were talking to her in some foreign language that only she seemed to understand. The thought of her poor child being raised by a junkie whore and a convicted pervert made his skin crawl. Whacking this bitch would give the child a chance at a better life he thought to himself. The baby would be adopted out and grow up with decent folk. Son of a Bith, she was too easy. He could hack off her fucking head and she probably wouldn't even know it until they told her when she arrived in Hell. Walking up behind her, The Clownfather took his knife and went straight for her jugular, her blood flowed into the punch bowl, He was right. The dumb bitch didn't even know what hit her.

Father O'Shea's turn! Nunzio had padlocked all the doors to the Social Hall, there was no way out.. The Good Shepard witnessed all the carnage, all the blood splattered on his pristine hall. All things done in the dark were being brought into the light by The Clownfather.

"Son, it's not too late for you to find redemption. To find absolution. I know who you are behind the mask of make up that you wear. God knows who you are, he sees all, he sees all. He knows your soul, " Father O'Shea called out to Nunzio in his booming voice.

"That's right Father O'Shea , he does see all. He knows your soul. He sees the things you do in the dark. The games you play with weak drug addicted mothers who need a fix. God sees all. He sees you get drunk, break your vows. Put one face on to the world and another one on behind closed doors. I see all too, " Nunzio retorted.

"Give me the knife son, " Father O'Shea commanded.

The lights went out and scurrying of footsteps in the Social Hall could be heard.

Father O'Shea did get the knife, his neck was sliced from side to side. A smile was carved out on his face. The knife was plunged in his heart after his manhood was crudely chopped from his person and tucked in his collar. A Note was left by his body that read ' All things done in the dark are brought into the light'. The Clownfather was nowhere to be found.

TASTE THE RAINBOW by Lisa Dabrowski©

Betty, a petite and unassuming honey blonde homemaker spent her days quietly at home. She was in her late twenties, married to a Marketing Executive , and spent her days taking care of their home in the quiet suburb while he earned a substantial living in the city.

Betty cooked casseroles, scrubbed foors, vacuumed carpets. She did whatever it took to keep busy. Gardening, planting flowers. Keeping up appearances in the suburbs was essential. All the beautiful people live in the suburbs, everything is perfect on the outside.

Retreating to the tranquility of her bedroom, she thought perhaps she might take a respite for awhile and watch a little television. Poised on her bed, she began channel surfing and stopped when she heard a woman screaming. This wasn't any ordinary scream, this was a rapturous scream. One filled with sweet ecstacy and torturous selight. Her interest was piqued immediately. She surveyed the room , making sure the blinds were drawn. Heaven forbid the neighbors should see this. The woman was being fucked twenty ways from Sunday by what appeared to be a clown. Yes it was most definitely a clown. The clown then pulled his ten inch one eyed monster out and spewed his jizz into her open mouth. It dripped down her chin! Betty was shocked, She was shocked at how wet she had become and found herself with her hand down her pants, masturbating vigorously. She had an orgasm so big, she drenched the bed with her juices.

She cleaned up the bed, changed the sheets, and showered. She could not get the Clowns out of her mind. She felt like a jittery alkie in need of a drink. She must have more. She resolved to drive into the city and pick up some adult books on Clowns, The trip was justified in her mind with a decision to do some grocery shopping as well.

Betty was ashamed to go to the Adult Store. She parked around the corner and walked. Inside she browsed around. She saw all sorts of things that she had never even dreamed of before. Perhaps it was ignorance or innocence, she was a virgin when she married. She grew up in the country, and sex was not a subject spoken of much. It was considered ill mannered or evil. They were church going people. Bible Thumpers in her little hometown. Her parents told her she was cursed because she was baren. Betty and her husband Steve got married and moved to the city after graduation, and never looked back.

"Do you need some help with anything , sunshine?" asked a cheerful woman behind the counter, with a cigarette hanging out of her mouth.

Startled back into reality, Betty replied, " I was watching this movie on TV about Clowns and ,"

" You are into Clown Porn! I have just the thing for you Sunshine. It's a book called Taste The Rainbow. All kinds of Clown Porn in there from Bukkake to Butt Sex! Shall I ring it up for you?" The woman asked.

Not even sure what the woman was talking about, Betty agreed to purchase the book. She was still reeling from embarrassment and hoped that none of her husband's friend's saw her coming in there. The woman threw a vibrator in the bag as well. A rainbow coloured one. Betty thought that odd, perhaps they had an overstock and were trying to get rid of them.

A week had come and gone. Betty had grown into the routine of doing her chores by day, and by night , as her husband Steve lay there snoring next to her, she would pull out her book Taste The Rainbow. Masturbating to all the Clowns spewing their spunk on the pages in between. Fantasizing that it was her. Hoping against hope that one day she would get to say " Jizz, it's what's for dinner!" or 'Throw another Cream Pie my way!" She was addicted to the clowns, she couldn't even have sex with her husband anymore without fantasizing that a Clown was standing above her spewing his spunk onto her forehead as her husband pumped her. Bathing in Clown jizz, that was her dream, to taste it, to feel it, to smell it, to become one with it. To truly taste the rainbow.

The next morning she was reading the paper with her coffee. Leaving it open on the table, she went to the fridge to get some strawberry jam for her toast, She dropped the jar on the floor when she noticed the advertisement for the Circus coming to the arena. Her heart raced. This could be her big chance. The opportunity of a lifetime. They were scheduled to be there next week. She had to find a way to sneak out and go. She couldn't live her life without tasting the rainbow.

Betty could barely contain herself at dinner that evening. She squirmed about all through supper, restless and on the edge of her seat, her husband Steve making small talk , mentioned that the Circus was coming to town. Betty felt her knees go weak. She felt a flush to her face as heat rushed to her bottom, and thought for sure that she was going to faint as the room began to spin. She had got what her grandmother used to call a case of the vapors. Her trembling hand grasped the ice water and put it to her lips.

"Darling, are you okay, " Steve asked, noticing his wife's behaviour. He waled over to her and put his arms around her. " There, there, sweetheart. Clowns are nothing to be afraid of. The Circus also has animals, it can be a fun experience. I know we were discouraged from doing frivolous things that brought us pleasure when we were kids, but we have escaped from that place, Look around, honey. We have a good life today, " he said and planted a sweet kiss upon her cheek.

Steve's sentiment only added to her feelings of guilt and angst at wanting to live out her fantasies. How could she betray the man who had rescued her from a life of hellish punishments. A life lived without any love. She owed everything to Steve and to her marriage. How could she turn her back on her marriage, for one night of jizz filled passion with Clowns? Her mind and heart were in turmoil, but her lust raged on. She felt deep inside that she needed to become a Clown Slut , if only for one night, to sow her wild oats, so to speak, just to get it out of her system.

Later that night, after Steve had went to bed, She logged onto her computer and pre-ordered tickets to the Circus. She became so excited that she began to drip. The thought of her fantasy coming to fruition was just too good to be true. She wenti into the bathroom with her book, Taste The Rainbow, and her Rainbow couloured vibrator and began to masturbate while looking at images of the clown sluts getting loads of cum spewed in their face. Thick , rich, ribbons of jizz sprayed in their face. They were covered in it. The Jizz must have flowed from them like soft serve vanilla ice cream, She so wanted to feel it. To bathe in it. To be engulfed in it. Turning the vibrator on high speed she had a tumultuous orgasm that rocked her inner being.

The night of the Circus had finally arrived. Betty felt like a child on the Eve of Christmas. She was full of expectations.. She was filled with wonder and joy. She could hardly contain herself waiting for the time to go. She thought to herself, this must be what groupies feel like when they go to the concerts of the Heavy Metal Rock Stars. Pumped full of adrenalin, the wet panty syndrome, in total worship and adoration for the object of their affection. She was now a Clown Groupie. She worshipped the Rainbow phallus and the jizz that flowed from it was the true object of her affection.

Watching the Circus she was titillated . She enjoyed the Big Top Extravaganza. Lion Tamers, Fire Eaters, and Magicians. Elepahants and monkeys too graced the rings. Acrobats astounded the crowd with their graceful agility. The precion of the Tight Rope Walkers was heart stopping to say the very least. The Ringmaster was dashing if not downright dapper in his suit, commanding the show. She wasn't here for them though, infact they were a mere distraction from the main attraction and in her mind, the real stars of the show The Clowns. Yes, she thought to herself, send in the clowns.

Finally the moment she had been waiting for, the clowns were being announced. A rainbow coloured car and a fire engine pulled up into the center ring. A car load of mayhem piled out of the tiny clown car. Horns were being honked, dancing was happening haphazardly. The hose on the fire engine was being sprayed, but pink foam was coming out everywhere. A loathsome mess. A rather tall clown dressed in a black suit with a purple wig and a green nose slipped in the foam, and was helped up by an identically clad Clown of shorter stature. Pies were flung about. Cream Pies.! This was spectacular, she thought to herself, and made her loins quiver.

All good things must come to an end, or do they? The Circus was over for the night, but if she could find a way to get backstage to the Clowns, perhaps the fun didn't have to end, but could begin. She began to survey the arena. Glancing around she saw the "Event Staff Only" Entrance. This must be where she would have to sneak in. Casually she entered through the door. She was hoping that no one would notice she didn't belong there. The humiliation of being ejected by security wouldn't even begin to match the hurt she would feel at not being able to get close to living out her fantasy.

She had made it. This was too good to be true. She was standing outside the dressing room of The Clowns. She could hardly contain herself. She needed to find a way inside with out looking like the stalker she really was. She peered into the room a little closer, and recognized one of the clowns from the book Taste The Rainbow. She couldn't contain herself any longer, and let out a squeal of delight.

Her pulse quickened as she felt their eyes upon her. She had been caught, standing there in the Dressing Room doorway of The Clowns with a copy of Taste The Rainbow clutched in her hand, drool dripping from the corner of her mouth. She was leering at them, but wait a minute , what was this? They were leering back at her!

"Come in Toots, and shut the door behind you, " The Clown in the chair said to her.

Betty couldn't believe this was happening to her. She had fantasized about this encounter all week. Meeting The Troop of Clowns was all that occupied her mind from the first time she heard the Circus was coming to the city. Reality or Sureality? Either way it didn't matter to Betty, she was close to them now, and being close to the clowns meant she was one step closer to tasting the rainbow.

"What's your name Toots?" asked the tall clown.

"Betty," she answered with a giggle and wiggle.

"You're a cute little girl, Betty. Did you come here to play?" asked a clown in a pink wing with a gruff voice.

Betty was dancing about , her stiffened nipples protruding from her blouse. Electrical impulses tingled through out her body. She was more turned on than she had ever been in her entire life. She could actually feel her juices flowing from over stimulated cunt.

" I came here to taste the rainbow, " Betty replied, looking down.

The Clowns formed a huddle and were whispering something, leaving Betty standing by the door waiting hopelessly like a love sick puppy. Actually she was more like a Bitch in heat. Yes that is a better picture of her.

"Ready for some fun?" collectively they asked Betty.

" Oh, yes. I am so ready!" she exclaimed.

They grabbed her by the hand and took her into the next room. Her eyes were big as saucers. One of them explained to her that this was their Whack Room, where they came to blow off steam. They had blown off quite a bit of steam. There were a couple of olde time fire extinguishers, that were filled with a white substance. Her heart began to race wildly when they asked her if she would disrobe for them. She was a beauty. Curves that went all day long. Ample breasts, a plush round bottom, juicy thighs, and a dripping cunt. Skin as smooth as spun silk. Blue eyes that were as deep as the ocean and lovely locks of honey blonde hair. Making this doll taste the rainbow was going to be a pleasure indeed.

The short clown , lunged at her dripping cunt. French kissing it with his tongue. Lapping up her juices like a dog. Suckling on her clit as if he were giving it a blow job. In and out his tongue rolled around in her sweet mound delighting in her nectar, her juices squirting like a fountain. She screamed in the agony of ecstacy. He was persistent. Fucking her cunt with his tongue, she thrusting back. Clowns stood on each side of her masturbating on her nipples, the sensation was amazing, the tip of their cock grazing her erect nipple added to her pleasure, their precum dripping, then all at once they shot their wad all over breasts. Ribbons, upon ribbons of endless jizz flowing down her cleavage. Her cunt still being ravaged away. She was in Nirvana. The Tall Clown took the fire extinguisher, full of jizz, and sprayed her down with it. From head to toe. She was covered In Jizz. Then he took his leaking cock and put it in her screaming mouth, and shot his load down her throat.

She had Tasted The Rainbow! She was enrobed in it, engulfed in it. Her Fantasy was fulfilled that day.

Betty lay there squirming about on the table, still reeling from orgasmic delight and the wonder of it all. The Clowns weren't through playing with her yet. They realized that she was indeed a slut, A Clown Hoe, and she needed to be taught a lesson, no matter how severe it may be. She had her fun, now it was time to pay the price for it.

One of the troop clicked on a flashing strobe light, changing up the already chaotic mood in the room. Spheres of variant hues flashed upon Betty, changing her complexion in from pristine white to crimson rouge in literally milliseconds. She was becoming a bit faint at sights, and now at the distorted blaring of Send In The Clowns . Tasting the Rainbow was taking on a new meaning as she felt she was becoming The Rainbow.

"Ready for your Cream Pie?' One of them asked leering at her, placing what appeared to be a squirt gun to her head.

The squirt gun, loaded with jizz, was placed in her mouth, as the clown mounted her. One by one, each of the clowns had their way with her. Roughly pumping her, shouting obscenities at her while shoving their monstrous clown cocks in and out of hole. She was no longer tasting the Rainbow, The Rainbow was Tasting Her. She was in agony.

Betty lay there in a near catatonic state. The lights forming prisms in the tears that stream down her face. A small town girl, discovering her sexual perversions, had indeed turned out to be a true perversion. Her husband was not there to rescue her now, perhaps her family was right in shunning her. Look at the mess she had become from being a greedy cumslut. Did Steve bring her out of the sticks for this? Was this how she repaid him for giving her a good life?

Betty was jolted back into reality when she heard The Clowns open the door and address someone as "The Clownfather".

"We did as you commanded, Clownfather, " said the Tall Clown.

"Very good. I am pleased. I have tried to settle down with this one, but you see, she has proved to me that all of them are liars, sluts and whores. She was given a test of loyalty, and failed. Tasting the Rainbow was more important to the cumslut, little did she realize that she had the rainbow all along., " The Clownfather replied.

Betty trembled inside, she recognized that voice. It was Steve. She knew he was adopted by a family in their small town, but had no idea of his origins, he always told her that his real parents were dead.

How could he have concealed such a secret from her for their entire marriage?

Dressed in the Frock of a Priest, white collar and all, full clown face, The Clownfather approached Betty. The lights flashing on him only made him more ominous.

He leaned down to her, in his hand was a shiny butcher knife. She could see her eyes in the blade of the knife. She could see her own fear and betrayal staring back at her.

"Steve, I am ,"Betty started, but was interrupted when The Clownfather put The knife over her mouth.

"You are such a disloyal cumslut!" He said finishing the line for her. " I tried hard to be Steve, but Steve is not here right now. I am The Clownfather. I learned as a child that people do most of their evil deeds while hiding behind a mask. They wear a mask to hide their ugly deeds that they do in the dark. They are shameless, and they know no real loyalty to anyone but their own selfish desires. Much like you, Betty," he said looking down at her.

Tears of A Clown began to play softly in the room The Tall Clown came in with Super Soaker Squirt Gun fully loaded with jizz. He placed the barrel in Betty's mouth. The Clownfather took his knife and placed it to her throat. The trigger was pulled on the gun, Betty was guzzling jizz so fast, she was choking on it.

Looking down at Betty and what a cumslut she had become, The Clownfather realized he didn't have a choice but to put the blade to her neck. Her disloyalty proved it . Placing the tip of the bade at her jugular, as she struggled and choked on jizz, with one deft swipe, he slit her throat, and she bled out.

"Feed her to the lions, boys, " The Clownfather said before leaving the room.

SCARS OF LOVE©

He proudly wears

The scars of love

Deftly left in his back

Left over from love

The night before

Pleasure she took

Desires he fulfilled

Comfort in the sting

Found from the thin line

All in the name of Love

SINFUK ©

primal urges

give way

to

lustful purges

from sinfuks

deep within

the othermind

taking you higher

than a syringe could

pounding your taboo

giving you everything

moonpies and nectar

from gods and goddesses

revel in the sin

of the dark night

brothers and sisters

bayou babies gone bad

there is no black

there is no white

only the lust laden red

dripping down

the sweat of your

red hot sinfuk

FATHER JOHNSON VISITS SOUTHWICK MANOR

_Brother Johnson was on his weekly trek up the winding road that led to Southwick Manor to call upon Mistress Jayne for tea Southwick Manor loomed high atop the hillside, and the village folk often gossiped about Miss Jayne. Their innuendos ran rampant, with stories of wild orgies and witchcraft abound.

Truth be told, Brother Johnson was coming up the hill for more than a spot of tea. He was captivated by Mistress Jayne, so much so, that he had broken the very vows he held so sacred.

Brother Johnson rapped on the door gently. He could hear her stilettos clicking across the floor. His heart beat faster and faster.

"Come in, Darling," Said a curvy auburn haired woman in her late thirties, with fine porcelain skin.

"Yes, Mistress Jayne," he said walking through the threshold.

" Come sit by the fire with me, Brother Johnson, " she said walking over to the settee by the fireplace.

Pouring two cups of tea, she ran her hell up and down the length of his inner leg.

"Some sugar?" she asked , staring deeply into his eyes.

He was mesmerized. Sugar? There's only one kind of sugar I can think of right now. Thoughts raced through his head . He had to have her.

Tousling her fingers playfully through his hair, she led him to where he wanted to be. The sweet spot. Like honey he lapped at her. Juices flowing like nectar from the Gods into his mouth. She pushed her fleshy mound up into his mouth, and he devoured every drop of her as if she were a ripe peach. Fountains spew forth from her, as she pulled his hair.

Mistress Jayne pulled him up into her, where he began to slowly take her. Inching his way in, gliding, she felt like a wet and wild wonderland to him and he was in awe of her beauty. Suckling her erect nipples, he began to intensify his intrusiveness, going in as deep as he could go. He began to pound her with furious long strides, and she grabbed his belt and began flogging him with it. This appeared to add to his pleasure, He moaned, and she bucked , flogging harder and faster, moving her body in perfect rhythm with his. Eventually exploding in a fiery culmination of orgasmic bliss.

FATHER JOHNSON GIVES UP ABSTINENCE FOR LENT

_It had been nearly three months since Brother Johnson had found the time to visit Southwick Manor, and pay a call upon Mistress Jayne. He found himself quite busy now with the Lenten season upon him, but knew that he must find time to slip away and make the trek up the long and winding road to Southwick Manor to see Mistress Jayne.

One evening after the church was shut down for the night, Brother Johnson decided it was time for him to make his journey. Up the winding road he traversed, careful of the stones in the road. His mind wandered aimlessly with thoughts of how to approach Mistress Jayne. Would he just come right out and ask her to relieve his suffering, or after a glass of wine would he slip it into the conversation? What was it about her that he could not give up, that drove him to break his vows? He pondered this question until he came upon the door of Southwick Manor.

Knocking gently on the door, he thought perhaps he should just turn tail and run back to the church. He stood there frozen, as he heard her footsteps click clack across the room and inch closer to the door.

"Brother Johnson, please come in, " Mistress Jayne said upon opening the door.

He walked in and she seated him in next to fire, where she received her guests.

"To what do I have this honour, " she teased, running her fingers through his hair.

"Mistress Jayne, I needed to see you, " He answered sheepishly.

" I Haven't seen you for three months. Have you come to tell me what you have given up for Lent?
She asked, while stroking his inner thigh.

"I have given up abstinence for Lent, " he answered.

Mistress Jayne laughed wildly. "You have given up abstinence for Lent! Very well, I suppose you need to be flogged for this choice as well?"

"Yes, Mistress," he answered handing her his belt, and kneeling naked before her.

Mistress Jayne whipped Brother Johnson with his belt as he assumed the position of her oral slave. He tenderly licked her womanhood, lapping at it like a hungry dog laps at a sweet treat. He gorged himself upon her femininity, swallowing every drop that sprang forth from her as she writhed under him, flowing juices like a three tiered fountain.

Forming a collared leash around his neck, she pulled him up to her. "Take you release, and end your abstinence!" She commanded , drawing him inside of her. She pushed her fleshy mound up to meet him, grinding and rocking. He suckled her nipples, heightening her pleasure. Taking he fingernails she clawed up his back in the throes of passion, his back already bloody from the belt whipping.

"Give it to me!" she screamed.

Brother Johnson exploded within her, shooting fiery ribbons and streams within in her. He was abstinen

Resurrecting Elise

Richard and Marie lived an arranged marriage. Marie brought quite a substantial dowry to the pairing which made her an attractive catch to Richard. Land and money have a way of putting the words "I do" upon even the most reluctant of grooms.

The couple settled down in Orleans Parish steadfastly making use of an elegant and spacious manor her family had given them upon her marriage. Richard was a Trader for a Shipping Company. He often spent his days dockside overseeing and tracking orders that came and went through the port. Marie stayed home and tended to the social calendar, and maintenance of house staff.

Richard and Marie were invited to the theatre by friends to celebrate their Wedding Anniversary. Marie was delighted to be able to spend the evening out with her husband and to get away from the Manor House. Richard paid her no attention if truth be told, and she was chomping at the bit for any scrap of affection that he would toss her way. Perhaps tonight would be the night he would make love to her, it had been nearly six months since he had shared a bed with her. She was sure that this was not the way that couples behaved after five years of marriage. She often wondered if Richard married her soley for the money, if there was ever a spark of love or romance there to begin with.

A captivating songstress took the stage that night . Her raven tresses of hair spilling down upon her swollen bosom as she sweetly tweeted the songs. Her name was Elise and the magic of her beauty and voice and entranced Richard. He felt a stirring both in his soul and nether regions. He had to convince this rare songbird to be his. After the show Richard went to Elise to congratulate her on a superb performance, kissing her hand, shockwaves traveled through him as his glanced up to meet hers. He knew that she felt the chemistry between them. Perhaps she felt his power, and his wealth., for she did not need too much convincing to leave her tour and be kept by Richard.

Richard and Elise set up housekeeping in the French Quarter. Richard was so smitten with his songstress that he gave not a care to the idle gossip and innuendo that spread through society about his Mistress. His soul was kissed by hers and was a flame with a fire the likes of which he had never known. Three months into their affair , Elise went to him with the news of an impending birth. Their child.. Richard felt great pride swell within him, perhaps she would give him a son to carry on the family name. Then reality set in. He was still married to Marie! No child of his was going to be born a bastard! Something had to be done about Marie, and quickly.

Richard procured some arsenic from the shipyards that they used to for exterminating rats. This would surely exterminate a wife, he thought to himself. He went into the wine cellar, grabbed a nice carafe of Marie's favourite Bordeaux , and slipped a wee bit of arsenic into it, not enough for her to taste it, but surely enough for her to feel it. Clutching the bottle up under his arm, he went into the parlor with two glasses and offered Marie a toast to happier days. Explaining that his wandering days were over, kneeling beside her, kissing her hand and begging her forgiveness. Desperate for attention and affections Marie believed her husband and took the glass, it was her favourite, such a lovely gesture. Within minutes Marie lay retching on the floor. Gasping her final breath of life. Richard had accomplished what he had set out to do.

Realizing he hadn't much time to waste, Richard quickly moved Elise into the Manor House. Deeply in love as he was, he didn't care how it looked that a proper period of mourning was not kept. Elise had become his new bride, much to the dismay of the social community. Richard assumed that in time, the scandal would fade and both their marriage and is child would be accepted into society with open arms.

Elise did not fair well in the Manor House. Pregnancy was taking it's toll on her. She grew paler by the day. Her nausea had given way to violent bouts of morning sickness which apparently lasted all day, leaving her faint and anemic. The doctor prescribed bed rest for her. Richard feared this was payback for what he had done to Marie. He could not stand to see his beloved so ill.

The day came when Elise went into labour. Richard sent for the doctor straight away, he was taking no chances with the woman he loved. Outside the room he could hear her cries of agony and pain, he thought to himself that soon this will all be over and I will have My Sweet Elise back. Screams! He heard a Gasping Screams come from the nursemaid attending the Doctor. He peered into the room. There was blood everywhere. His soulmate laying there in a puddle of blood, dripping down onto the floor like a river. Wait a minute, he didn't hear a baby crying either. He glanced over at the Doctor, who was holding his son. A son with a freakishly blue pallor, that was unearthly still, and not breathing! They had both perished. Richard did not know whether to scream, cry or faint.

Richard remembered The Necromancer who lived in The French Quarter. Running from Elise's room he went to his horse and took a trip to his house. He felt certain that if anyone could bring his beloved back it would be him, He was prepared to pay a handsome sum as well, taking with him fifty pieces of gold, he knew that he could persuade The Necromancer to return to The Manor House with him. Richard was right, the gold did the trick, and he and The Necromancer made haste for The Manor House. The Necromancer assured Richard that this should be an easy feat since Elise had recently passed, bringing her back should only take a few incantations and spells. Drawing forth and summoning spirits, The Necromancer went to work on Elise's body. Incantations, lighting the wicks of two blue candles, The Necromancer called out the spirit of the one who had passed through no fault of her own. Summoning back the spirit of the wife who's only crime was love. The flames from the candles rose high in the air, an eerie blue light surrounded the bed. Elise opened her eyes and stared into those of the Necromancer. The Necromancer kissed her hand. Richard was so elated that he gave him an extra fifty gold pieces before he sent him on his way in one of his carriages.

Elise smiled at Richard and reached for his hand, demurely taking it. She was such a petite creature, one of the characteristics Richard adored about her. Kissing her hand , He leaned in to tell her that not even the chains of death could separate a love as true as theirs, and that he would go to any lengths to have her in his life. Just then she sat up in the bed, and put her arms gingerly around him, kissing his neck. Placing her hands upon his shoulders she glared into his eyes with a fire he had never witnessed from her before. Terror rose in the heart of Richard as he realised this was not his beloved songstress, but Marie! Paralyzed with fear, his mouth a jar, not a shriek able to escape his jowls Her hands went for his neck as she choked the life out of him before he slumped to the ground. She cackled the laugh of a mad woman,shrieking "Til death do us part!"

DR. SADISTIC WORLD HUNGER

DR. SADISTIC WAS CALLED IN BY THE FDA TO ASSIST THEM IN THEIR CLONING PROJECT. THEY WERE VERY EAGER TO INCREASE THE WORLD'S FOOD SUPPLY AND ATTEMPT TO ERADICATE ILLNESS SPREAD THROUGH MEAT AND MEAT BY-PRODUCTS.
AT ONCE HE SET UP HIS LABORATORY, TAKING GREAT CARE TO KEEP SEPARATE THE PETRI DISHES OF THE VARIOUS ANIMALS HE WOULD BE DUPLICATING. HE HAD ONE FOR CATTLE, ONE FOR SWINE, ONE FOR CHICKEN , ONE FOR LAMB, AND YES HE HAD DECIDED HE WOULD CLONE HUMANS AS WELL.

HE ACHIEVED GREAT SUCCESS WITH THE CHICKEN AND IT WAS TRICKLED INTO MARKET BY A MAJOR SUPPLIER , LABELED AS NATURALLY GROWN WITHOUT ANY ADDITIVES. THIS WAS TRUE TO A CERTAIN EXTENT,.THERE WERE NO STEROIDS OR HORMONES IN DR. SADISTIC'S CHICKENS, THEY CAME OUT AS EXACT DUPLICATES OF THE ORIGINAL CHICKEN HE HAD TAKEN THE DNA FROM. THE CHICKENS WERE A WIN/WIN FOR EVERYONE INVOLVED. THE GOVERNMENT WAS PLEASED WITH DR. SADISTIC'S WORK AND GAVE HIM ADDITIONAL FUNDING AND THE GREENLIGHT TO GO AHEAD WITH ANY FURTHER CLONING PROCEDURES HE DEEMED SUITABLE.

DR. SADISTIC ENJOYED HIS ROLE OF PLAYING GOD IN THE LABORATORY. HE HAD DECIDED THAT PERHAPS HE WOULD CROSSBREED THE LAMB AND SWINE. HE CHUCKLED TO HIMSELF HOW IT COULD BE MARKETED AS KOSHER AND NON-KOSHER AS WELL . OF COURSE THE ANIMAL WAS TRULY AN ABOMINATION, BUT DID SURVIVE LONG ENOUGH TO MAKE IT TO THE GRINDHOUSE. THE DR. FIGURED THAT WITH THE RIGHT SEASONINGS AND CURING PROCESSES NO ONE WOULD BE ABLE TO TELL THE DIFFERENCE, AND NO ONE COULD. HE HAD ACHIEVED ANOTHER MIRACLE FOR THE GOVERNMENT.
THE PRICE OF CATTLE HAD BEEN RISING BEYOND BELIEF, PERHAPS IT HAD BEEN THE WAY PEOPLE HAD BEEN HIT HARD WITH MAD COW DISEASE, OR MAYBE IT WAS ALL OF THOSE DAMNED OIL RANCHERS IN TEXAS RAISING UP THE PRICES. EITHER WAY, SOMETHING HAD TO BE DONE.

DR. SADISTIC SET OUT TO CLONE CATTLE. EXTRACTING DNA FROM A PRIZE STEER, HE CAREFULLY PLACED THE CELLS IN THE PETRI DISH, WHEN HE PRICKED HIS FINGER, AND A DROPLET OF HIS BLOOD FELL INTO THE DISH. IT OCCURRED TO HIM THAT THIS WAS THE PERFECT OPPORTUNITY TO CROSSBREED HUMANS WITH CATTLE. HE KEPT A FAR CLOSER EYE ON THIS EXPERIMENT THAN THE OTHER ONES, BEING THAT HE WAS VESTED PERSONALLY IN IT. THE BEAST HAD GROWN TO BE GROTESQUE IN NATURE. A HUMAN HEAD, WITH HORNS, A BODY OF STEER, THE LEGS OF AN ANIMAL COVERED IN HIDE AND HAIR AND THE FEET WERE CLOVEN. THE EYES WERE AS GREEN AS HIS. A TRUE MONSTROSITY. HIS CHEST SWELLED WITH PRIDE.
AT ONCE HE SENT THE CREATURE TO THE GRINDHOUSE, MAKING PATTIES OF IT FOR CONSUMPTION.
A PRESS CONFERENCE WAS HELD UNVEILING THE PATTIES.

DR. SADISTIC CHUCKLED TO HIMSELF AS HE WATCHED THEM EAT HIS CREATION.

FLOPPY DICK APOCALYPSE

_The Clownfather, who by this time had assembled his own mob of organized Clowns willing to do his bidding was seeking a way to infiltrate the government. His Domme, Mistress Rosie, had a few connections in politics, and offered to share them with him.

Along with the help of Mistress Rosie's pet, Dr. Sadistic, an alliance was made with The Filthy Whore on Capitol Hill. Dr. Sadistic had developed a drug that would render a man impotent. This drug would have the opposite effect on women increasing their libidos. Dubbed as "Floppy Dick" by Dr. Sadistic, this drug would be introduced into the water supply of the United States, and would affect and inflict the entire nation.

Misery and mayhem would ensue. Chaos, it would be a nightmare. The nation, under sexual duress and repression would literally run to their doctors for a miracle drug.

Sex, drugs and money. Music to both the government's and The Clown father's ears. An alliance was formed.

After about two weeks of the contaminated water supply being distributed, it happened. A nightmare fell upon the America. The Floppy Dick Apocalypse had arrived. Insatiable women caught in the throes of cat scratch fever with men unable to achieve an erection. Sheer torture. A nightmare. Just as projected they ran in droves to their doctors to get prescriptions for the magic pill developed by Dr. Sadistic.

www.ingramcontent.com/pod-product-compliance
Lightning Source LLC
Chambersburg PA
CBHW080905120626
46555CB00008B/2959